School Play

More Super ♡ Duper ♡ Royal ♡ Deluxe books!

Missy's
Super ♥ Duper ♥ Royal ♥ Deluxe

School Play

By
Susan Nees

BRANCHES

SCHOLASTIC INC.

For Anna

No part of this work may be reproduced, stored in a retrieval system, or transmitted in any form or by any means, electronic, mechanical, photocopying, recording, or otherwise, without written permission of the publisher. For information regarding permission, write to Scholastic Inc., Attention: Permissions Department, 557 Broadway, New York, NY 10012.

Library of Congress Cataloging-in-Publication Data

Nees, Susan, author, illustrator.
School play   written and illustrated by Susan Nees.
pages cm — (Missy's super duper royal deluxe ; 3)
Summary: The class is putting on a play about George Washington Carver, and Missy is mad because she does not have an important part, but when the lead actor freezes, Missy saves the play.
ISBN 978-0-545-49611-7 (hardcover) — ISBN 978-0-545-43853-7 (pbk.) 1. Children's theater—Juvenile fiction. 2. Temper tantrums—Juvenile fiction. 3. Elementary schools—Juvenile fiction. [1. Theater—Fiction. 2. Elementary schools—Fiction. 3. Schools—Fiction. 4. Emotions—Fiction.] I. Title.
PZ7.N384Sch 2013
[E]—dc23
                            2013011697

ISBN 978-0-545-49611-7 (hardcover) / ISBN 978-0-545-43853-7 (paperback)

12 11 10 9 8 7 6 5 4 3 2 1   13 14 15 16 17 18/0

Printed in China   38
First Scholastic printing, October 2013

Table of Contents

Chapter One
Rotten, Old Peanut

This is Melissa Abigail Rose.

But everyone calls her "Missy."

This is Missy's cat Pink.

Everyone calls him "Pink."

Missy has dreams. Big dreams.
She dreams of being a star.

I will have my own dressing room!

I will have a dessert named after me!

... do, re, mi, fa, so, la, ti, do ...

I will twirl in the spotlight!

THE NEW YORK TIMES

MISSY

I will be famous!

I will wear clothes that sparkle!

Missy dreams of being a star SO famous that she does not have to go to school when she does not want to.

Missy's mother could not understand why Missy did not want to go to school today.

But, Missy, today is your school play about George Washington Carver. You were really looking forward to it. Why don't you want to go?

Why?

I'll tell you why!

On <u>Monday</u>, my teacher, Miss Snodgrass, handed out our parts for the play. I got a rotten part! I got the part of A PEANUT!

On <u>Tuesday</u>, we got our lines for the play. I didn't get one single line! Can you believe it? A PEANUT WHO DOESN'T TALK!

On <u>Wednesday</u>, we had play practice. I found out there are lots of peanuts. And we all have to sing. So I am A PEANUT WHO DOESN'T TALK, BUT WHO SINGS!

THEN, on <u>Thursday</u>,
we got our costumes. I didn't get a fun
costume. I got a boring BROWN costume.
So I am a BORING, ROTTEN, OLD PEANUT
WHO DOESN'T TALK, BUT WHO SINGS
AND IS BROWN!

Now it is <u>Friday</u>. And I am . . .
NOT going to be a peanut,
NOT going to be in that play, and
NOT going to school today!

Chapter Two
Carver Shmarver

Quiet down. I know you are very excited about our George Washington Carver play today, but we have a busy day and blah, blah, blah . . .

When Missy got to school, she did not want to hear any more from Miss Snodgrass about the play. And she wanted to just forget about peanuts.

Let's take our seats.
It is time to share our
George Washington
Carver reports.
Who would like
to go first?

REPORTS?

12

Missy had forgotten about the report that was due today. Missy did not want to go first. Missy did not want to go at all! One by one, the other students shared their reports.

Alice made a mobile.

This is my George Washington Carver mobile. . . .

Tiffany brought peanut butter snacks.

George Washington Carver ate a lot of peanuts. . . .

Paulette made a drawing.

Here is George holding a peanut. . . .

Taylor made a map.

And he lived here. Or was it here?

Dexter made a model.

I made this out of peanuts.

Then it was Oscar's turn.

Oscar was not a talker. Oscar was a thinker. He just stood at the front of the classroom. He didn't say a word. Not one single word.

Oscar always had a rough time getting started. But once Oscar got going, he had oodles of interesting things to share.

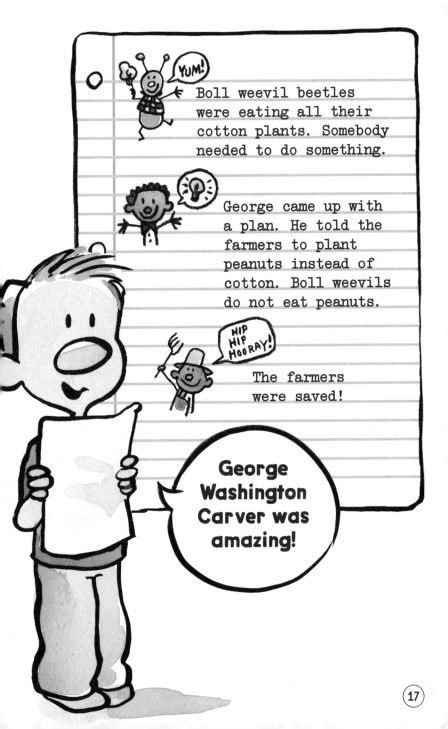

Oscar even brought in his insect collection to share. And there was a real boll weevil beetle in it.

DOODLE BUG

STINK BUG

CABBAGE BEETL

SNUG BUG

BUTTERFLY

FLUTTERBY

CRAWLER

MONKEY MOTH

LIL BUG

LEAF HOPPER

TWEEDLE BUG

TTLE BUG

BOLL WEEVIL BEETLE

WHOPPER

19

When it was Missy's turn, she walked to the front of the room. Even though she hadn't written her report, she did have a few things to share.

George Washington Carver was an important man. He invented peanuts and boll weevils. And also his face is on the dollar bill because he was our first president and . . .

. . . and I brought in this bar of soap that sort of looks like there's a face in it and —

Before Missy could finish, Miss Snodgrass stopped her.

Chapter Three
Twirl, Shuffle, and Clap

Missy's next class was Music. Miss Didi was the music teacher. Miss Didi talked loudly, waved her hands a lot, and used fancy words.

In Music, Missy liked to play the drums
and the recorder. She liked to play music
bingo, too.

drum

xylophone

ukulele

recorder

But today they weren't going to do any of
those things. Today, they were going to
practice for the school play.

While the other students went over their lines, the peanuts practiced their song and dance.

All right, peanuts! This is our last chance to rehearse before this afternoon's play.

And a one,

And a two,

And a one, two, three . . .

At first, Missy didn't feel like singing.

But when they got to her favorite part,
Missy joined right in.

LA LA LA LA LA!

Miss Didi said Missy was singing too loud.
Way too loud.

Next, the peanuts practiced their moves for the songs. But Missy's timing was off. When it was time to twirl, she shuffled.

When it was time to shuffle, she clapped.

And when it was time to clap, she twirled.

Miss Didi said she had the perfect place for Missy. She put Missy in the back row.

Missy was ready for Music to end. Lunch was next. Missy was ready for lunch. Missy was ready for a change.

Chapter Four
Meat Loaf

At lunchtime, things did change. They got worse. Much worse.

Missy couldn't find her lunchbox anywhere.
She wondered where it could be.

Missy had left her lunchbox on the school bus. No lunchbox meant no chocolate pudding! No orange smiles!

sandwich

orange smiles

juice box

chocolate pudding

No lunchbox meant Missy would have to eat . . .

. . . meat loaf and brussels sprouts!

Missy hated brussels sprouts, and she certainly didn't trust the meat loaf.

When Missy sat down, all everyone talked about was the play.

They talked . . .

... and they talked ...

. . . and they TALKED!

Just then, the bell rang. Missy's heart sank. It was time—time to put on her costume.

RING

RRING

All right, students. It's SHOWTIME!

Chapter Five
Lights. Places. ACTION!

While the audience took their seats, the students lined up backstage. The play was about to begin.

The students were told to keep their eyes and ears open.

Listen carefully. I will call you when it is your turn to go onstage. Be ready!

Then the play was under way.

Missy sat backstage and waited.

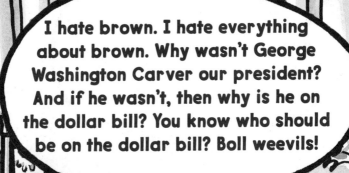

And maybe
a bow.

Do boll weevils
have horns?

These are
boll weevil boots!

How about a
Queen Boll Weevil?

Up, up, and away with Super Beetle!

Do boll weevils have tails?

Why isn't there a boll weevil in this play?

There should be at least one!

Missy watched as Oscar walked slowly onstage. Then he stopped. He stared out into the audience.

Chapter Six
A Little Bit of Sparkle

Umm . . .
Ahhh . . .
Umm . . .

BOLL
weev

Oscar was George Washington Carver.
This was his big scene. But he didn't say
a word. Not one single word.

When Oscar stopped, the entire play stopped. The cow didn't moo. The farmer's wife didn't know when to say her lines. The peanuts didn't dance and sing.

But Missy knew that once Oscar got going he would be fine. Somebody just needed to do something.

Missy smiled. She had a plan. This play
needed something special and Missy knew
exactly what it was. This play needed
some sparkle!

Missy the boll weevil twirled out from behind all the other peanuts. And she sparkled!

She shuffled over to Oscar.

Hello, George Washington Carver—the man who was a famous scientist and NOT our first president. I am Missy the boll weevil.

She clapped and sang and danced in the spotlight.

Missy was a star!

That was all it took. Just like that, the play was back on track.

Oscar said his lines.

Try planting peanuts.

BOLL WEEV

The cow remembered to moo.

MOO.

The farmer's wife knew when to say her lines.

P-p-peanuts?

And, as the curtain fell, Missy added
one last twirl. Because a little bit of
sparkle goes a long way.

Everyone agreed that not only
was this the best play ever,
it was—

Super Duper
Royal Deluxe!

The End

Susan Nees

grew up sharing the spotlight with five brothers and four sisters. When she was young, Susan loved the idea of being onstage. She would even put on "cooking shows" under the mulberry trees in the grove behind their house. Her favorite ingredients were dandelions, clover, mulberries, and mud. Today, Susan does not often find herself onstage, but like Missy, she does like to twirl, sparkle, and sing loudly. Susan lives in Georgia with her family. Missy's Super Duper Royal Deluxe is her first children's book series.